For my Jamesie —S.H.

Dedicated to my (not so) little brother Sheriph Adeola, I'm very proud of the father you've become and the brother you are. Love you dude. —D.A.

My Dad is a Grizzly Bear
This edition published in 2022 by
Red Comet Press, LLC, Brooklyn, NY

Originally published in 2021 by
Macmillan Children's Books an imprint of
Pan Macmillan, London, England

10 9 8 7 6 5 4 3 2 1

Library of Congress Control Number: 2021940825
ISBN (HB): 978-1-63655-011-4
ISBN (Ebook): 978-1-63655-012-1

Printed in China

RedCometPress.com

Written by
SWAPNA HADDOW

Illustrated by
DAPO ADEOLA

MY DAD IS A GRIZZLY BEAR

RED COMET PRESS • BROOKLYN

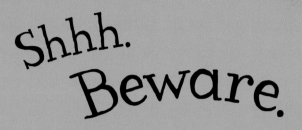

Shhh.
Beware.

My dad is a **grizzly bear.**

He has the fuzziest fur that **scratches** and **scritches.**

Mom laughs and teases him when he gives her big sloppy kisses.

He chases me and my sister, growling and waving his enormous paws, because he is a **grizzly bear.**

He eats all the honey in the house. It drips off his pancakes and sticks to his whiskers.

Drip.

Drip.

Driiiiiiip.

He never leaves any for me because he is a **grizzly bear.**

He naps all the time, anywhere, any place, day or night—in the car, in the pool, in the playground, and even in the movie theater.

Especially in the movie theater.

Sometimes he's asleep,
even when he's awake.

"Are you asleep, Dad?"

"Yes."

When he does wake up, he's so grumpy.
He **grumbles** and **grunts** and **stomps** around,
hunting for food, because he is a **grizzly bear.**

Sometimes on the weekend, Dad makes the whole family go for loooOOong walks in the woods, even when our legs are aching and our noses are frozen.

He's never cold because of all his thick **grizzly bear** fur.

Sometimes he catches fish in his **TEETH**.

Sometimes he climbs to the top of the **TALLEST** tree.

Sometimes he can run
FASTER than a bus.

And he has the
LOUDEST
growl.

All because he is a
grizzly bear.

One day, Dad packed
up the car and said,

**"We're going camping
in the woods."**

I hate camping.
The food is always soggy.
We always get lost.

And it *always* rains.

We had to eat our wet, mushy sandwiches under a tree while Dad set up our tent.

Dad was very happy, because he is a wood-dwelling **grizzly bear.**

At bedtime, Dad went for a wander in the woods, perhaps he was looking for his friends. Mom tried to cheer us up with a story.

It was all about . . .

a **grizzly bear.**

A **huge** grizzly bear.
A huge, **hairy,** very scary
grizzly bear.

Maybe my dad is
a bit **grumpy**,
and a bit **fuzzy.**

Maybe he does
eat all the honey.

And maybe he
would rather live
in the woods.

But when I'm scared,
there isn't anyone else
who can give me . . .

...the biggest, **warmest,** best ever

BEAR HUG!

My dad may be a **grizzly bear**,
but he's my favorite **grizzly bear**.
Besides, there are fiercer
things than bears . . .

Wait until you hear my mom

ROAR!

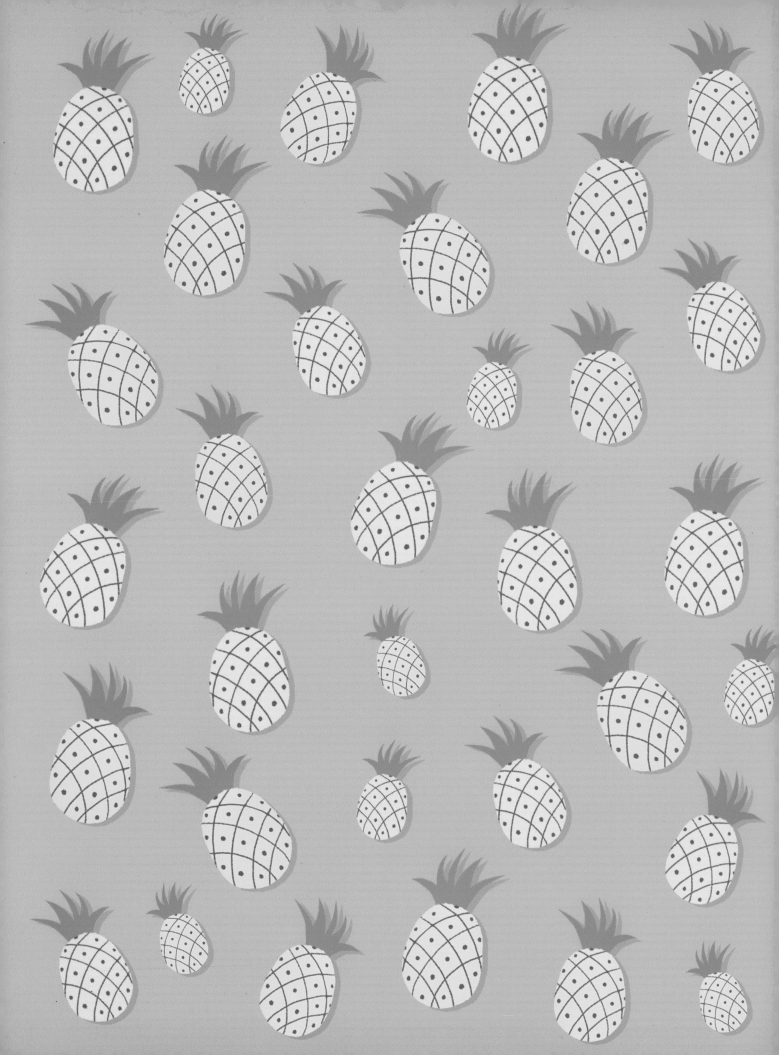